GUMDROP
GOES FISHING
Val Biro

ISBN 0 340 33801 6
First published 1984.   Copyright © 1984 by Val Biro
Published by Hodder and Stoughton Children's Books,
a division of Hodder and Stoughton Ltd, Mill Road, Dunton Green, Sevenoaks, Kent TN13 2YJ
Printed in Great Britain.   All rights reserved.

HODDER AND STOUGHTON
LONDON SYDNEY AUCKLAND TORONTO

'It would be nice to have fish for supper
tonight,' said Mr Oldcastle to his dog,
Horace. 'Tell you what – we'll take
Gumdrop down to the seaside and I'll do
a little fishing.'
Horace was very pleased to hear this. He
liked the seaside, and he liked fish.

A fine vintage car like Gumdrop needs polishing before it goes on a trip. So Mr Oldcastle polished the body and the wings, the radiator and the lamps, the thermometer and the horn.

Gumdrop sparkled in the sunshine as they set out, with rod and creel on the front seat and a fishing net tied firmly at the back.

Everybody waved as they saw this smart old car chugging along. 'Mind how you go!' they called, and 'Good luck!' A young lad shouted: 'Going fishing? Mind you don't drown that old crock!'

Mr Oldcastle resented that: Gumdrop was NOT an old crock! He was the smartest car that ever went to the seaside!

When they arrived, he parked Gumdrop right down on the beach. Horace felt a little sleepy because he had had a big breakfast, so Mr Oldcastle told him to lie on the floor of the car, and he put up the hood so that the dog could sleep more comfortably in the shade.

Horace was already snoring as Mr Oldcastle took his fishing rod and creel and walked across to the pier.

He settled down and began fishing. But there wasn't a fish in sight, nor a bite or a nibble on his hook. The fish must have been too lazy on that warm sunny day to come near the pier.

'We shan't have much fish for supper tonight,' he muttered – and feeling a little sleepy himself he shut his eyes.

It must have been some hours later that he woke up with a start. He thought that he heard Horace barking. So he looked round towards Gumdrop. The tide had come in and Gumdrop wasn't there! He jumped up and looked out to sea – and there was Gumdrop, out at sea and floating away!

What's more, Horace was standing on the top of the hood, still barking. 'Stop that car!' yelled Mr Oldcastle as he tore off his jersey and shoes.

To see Gumdrop and Horace floating on the waves was too much – he must rescue them himself. So he shut his eyes and jumped.

People on the beach must have heard his yell, and the lifeboat was soon on its way, coming straight for Mr Oldcastle. 'Not me!' he spluttered. 'Go and save that dog over there!'

But he was pulled on board just the same, still spluttering.

The lifeboat came alongside Gumdrop. Horace looked frightened standing there on the hood, but when he heard his name being called he jumped straight into Mr Oldcastle's arms. He was safe at last.

Now it was Gumdrop's turn to be rescued. The men attached a thick rope and towed him safely back to the beach. Everybody was soaking wet but thank goodness, there was no damage.

People on the beach cheered when they landed and Mr Oldcastle thanked the lifeboat-men for rescuing them all. In the warm sunshine they soon dried, and Mr Oldcastle managed to dry Gumdrop's engine too. All was well again.

Except that there would be no fish for supper.

It was then that Mr Oldcastle saw the fishing net tied to Gumdrop. He burst out laughing. For in the net he saw two big shiny silver fish!

'Good old Gumdrop!' he said. 'You went out fishing and we shall have fish for supper after all!'